W9-ACD-486

MATTIE'S LITTLE POSSUM PET

Books by
Ida Luttrell

Three Good Blankets
Be Nice to Marilyn
Mattie's Little Possum Pet

ATHENEUM   1993   NEW YORK

Maxwell Macmillan Canada   Maxwell Macmillan International
Toronto   *New York   Oxford   Singapore   Sydney*

MATTIE'S LITTLE POSSUM PET

by **Ida Luttrell** illustrated by **Betsy Lewin**

Text copyright © 1993 by Ida Luttrell
Illustrations copyright © 1993 by Betsy Lewin

All rights reserved. No part of this book may be reproduced
or transmitted in any form or by any means, electronic or
mechanical, including photocopying, recording, or by any
information storage and retrieval system, without permission
in writing from the Publisher.

Atheneum　　　　　　　*Maxwell Macmillan Canada, Inc.*
Macmillan Publishing Company　　*1200 Eglinton Avenue East*
866 Third Avenue　　　　　　*Suite 200*
New York, NY 10022　　*Don Mills, Ontario M3C 3N1*

Macmillan Publishing Company is part of the
Maxwell Communication Group of Companies.

First edition
Printed in Singapore
10　9　8　7　6　5　4　3　2　1
The text of this book is set in 16 point Euro Times Roman.
The illustrations are rendered in watercolors.

Library of Congress Cataloging-in-Publication Data
Luttrell, Ida.
Mattie's little possum pet / Ida Luttrell; illustrated by Betsy
Lewin. —1st ed.
p.　cm.
Summary: Mattie takes in a possum and then mistakenly blames her
cat Prowler and her dog Howler for the messes he makes.
ISBN 0-689-31786-7
[1. Opossums—Fiction.　2. Pets—Fiction.]　I. Lewin, Betsy, ill.
II. Title.
PZ7.L97953Maw　1993
[E]—dc20　91-47709

To Hazel, Georgia, Bubs, and Alice,
and the ranch days
I. L.

For Rita Steinhauer
B. L.

L978m

Macmillan gift

9/1/93

One bright, leaf-tumbling morning Mattie grabbed her basket and went out the door.

"Here, Howler, come along, Prowler," she called to her dog and cat. "It's persimmon-picking time."

They passed the henhouse where her hens,
Dusty, Rusty, Ruffles, and Pearl, sang on their
nests.

"Singing hens are laying hens," Mattie said. "I'll
trade those eggs, the persimmons too, when I go to
the store."

And Mattie and Howler and Prowler started
down the path to the woods.

Suddenly Howler stopped. There on the path was a possum, toes to the sky, tongue out, and eyes rolled back in his head.

"Why, the poor little critter is hurt," said Mattie, putting it into her basket. Howler and Prowler leaped up to see.

"Down, now," said Mattie. "We'll take him home and make him well. We'll have a little possum pet."

Mattie hurried home with Howler and Prowler bumping at her heels. The possum peeped over the edge of the basket and made faces at Howler and Prowler.

"Hmpf!" said Howler. "Looks sound as a rock."

"Or a mule," said Prowler.

They followed Mattie into the kitchen. She set the basket on the floor and turned to warm some milk.

Howler and Prowler looked into the basket. The possum jerked Prowler's whiskers and thumped Howler's nose.

"Hey!" Howler yelled.

"Ouch!" Prowler wailed.

"Don't scare that baby," Mattie said.

The possum shook with silent laughter.

Mattie rushed to the possum and took it to her chair. She rocked and sang, "Dogs can be barky and rough. Cats can be picky and sly. But a possum pet is mighty sweet, as sweet as molasses pie."

"Disgusting," said Howler.

"Sickening," said Prowler.

The minute Mattie was out of sight the possum grinned and jumped out of bed. On nimble feet he darted across the room to the table. Sniffling and snuffling and looking for eggs, he knocked over the milk.

"Stay put!" Howler yelled, and went after the possum.

Skidding through the milk, Prowler rushed to help. The quick-footed possum hopped back into bed just as they heard Mattie's step on the porch.

Mattie opened the door and found Howler and Prowler in a puddle of milk and the possum sleeping sweetly in Howler's bed.

"Well, if this isn't a fine how-de-do!" said Mattie.

"No fair," cried Howler. "It was that possum."

"That possum pest!" added Prowler.

"Hush that barking and squalling and sit in that corner," said Mattie. "No eggs yet from Dusty and Pearl is worry enough. I don't need this mess and racket." Mattie put two eggs in a crock in the cupboard.

"Why can't you behave like the possum pet?"
she said. The possum snickered quietly, his nose
twitching and his tongue licking his shiny lips.

Prowler seethed and Howler steamed while
Mattie mopped the floor. Then Mattie picked up
her basket.

"Ripe persimmons won't wait," she said as she started out the door again.

Howler and Prowler jumped up to go too.

"You stay with the possum pet," said Mattie. "I can't leave him all by himself. No telling what might happen."

"You said it," Howler grumbled.

"And no romping in the house," Mattie said.

The screen door slammed behind her. The possum jumped out of bed again.

RETA E. KING LIBRARY
CHADRON STATE COLLEGE
CHADRON, NE 69337

"Stop him!" Howler yelled, and the chase was on. Around and around the house they ran, the possum bumping, jumping, and mattress-thumping across Mattie's bed.

He zipped past Howler and Prowler, and before they knew what had happened, the possum was swinging on the cupboard door.

"The eggs!" cried Prowler. She leaped for the cupboard and landed in the sink. By now the possum was slurping eggs and scattering shells.

"Up here," Howler bawled, and jumped onto the table.

Prowler sprang up, the possum scrambled down, and Mattie burst in yelling, "I hear a commotion!"

    Mattie saw Howler on the table, Prowler in the egg crock, and the possum asleep without a trace of egg on his face.

    "Beg mercy!" Mattie cried in a fury. "Eyes don't lie. I see an egg-snitching cat. And she's leading my dog astray to boot." And she grabbed Howler and Prowler and shoved them out the door.

"It pains me to part us,"
Mattie said, "but the man
at the store needs a mouser
and, Prowler cat, you're
it. I'll get my purse
and take you in."

"What did she say?" asked Prowler.

Howler's voice cracked. "It's the store for you. You are gone. Finished."

"I'll run away," cried Prowler, and she started across the porch.

"Wait," cried Howler. "Play dead."

So Prowler fell back, toes up, tongue out, and tail limp.

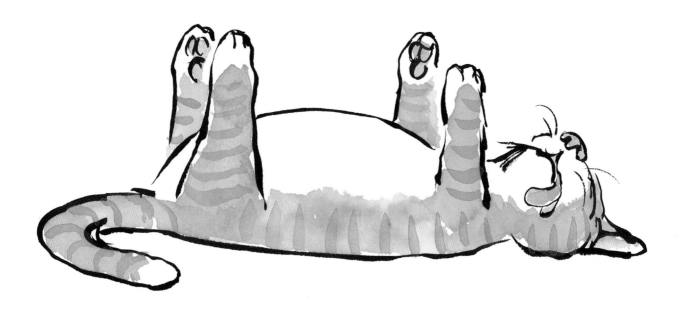

Mattie rushed out the door, then stopped short.

"My cat!" she cried. "Grief has done her in. I'll fetch some water and bring her to." And Mattie ran to the well.

The possum saw his chance and shot out of the house, into Dusty's nest. Dusty, Rusty, Ruffles, and Pearl exploded from the henhouse, shrieking, "A woolly-hopper egg popper!"

Mattie came running with a pail of water and found the possum gulping eggs.

"I'll be a scalded turnip. Why, you shifty little varmint!" she cried, and pitched the water at the possum.

Water splashed, feet thrashed, and the wet possum rolled himself into a lifeless lump.

"Oh no, you don't!" Mattie said. "That old trick won't work again."

Howler and Prowler watched gleefully as Mattie snatched the surprised possum by the scruff of the neck and hauled him off to the woods.

"Some pet!" she said when she returned. "To think I blamed my dog and cat."

And for the first time since they were babies, Mattie took Howler and Prowler and held them in her rocker.

"If you can forgive," she said as she rocked, "I can forget."